English edition: ©2018 CHOUETTE PUBLISHING (1987) INC.
Original title: *Wie doet dat toch?*
Text and illustrations: © Job, Joris and Marieke, 2016. All rights reserved.
First published by Uitgeverij Kluitman Alkmaar BV, The Netherlands, 2016.

Text and illustrations: Job, Joris and Marieke
Translation: Carine Laforest

CrackBoom! Books is an imprint of Chouette Publishing (1987) Inc.

Chouette Publishing would like to thank the Government of Canada and SODEC
for their financial support.

Bibliothèque et Archives nationales du Québec and Library and Archives Canada
cataloguing in publication

Roggeveen, Job, 1979-
[Wie doet dat toch? English]

Who did that?: a whodunit for children/written and illustrated by Job, Joris &
Marieke; translated by Carine Laforest.

(CrackBoom! Books)
Translation of: Wie doet dat toch?
Target audience: For children aged 3 and up.

ISBN 978-2-924786-38-3 (hardcover)

I. Oprins, Joris, 1980-, author, illustrator. II. Blaauw, Marieke, 1979-, author,
illustrator. III. Laforest, Carine, 1967-, translator. IV. Title. V. Title: Wie doet dat
toch? English.

PZ7.R633Wh 2018   j839.313'7   C2017-942514-5

CRACKBOOM! BOOKS

©2018 Chouette Publishing (1987) Inc.
1001 Lenoir St., Suite B-238
Montreal, Quebec H4C 2Z6 Canada
crackboombooks.com

Printed in Malaysia
10 9 8 7 6 5 4 3 2 1 CHO2022 DEC2017

WHO DID THAT?

A Whodunit for Children

Text and illustrations: Job, Joris and Marieke
Translation: Carine Laforest

CRACKBOOM!

The ruckus began with a broken seesaw.
It was cut in half.

But not only was the
seesaw broken,
Jeff's walking stick
was also in pieces.

Just like Bob's new
fishing rod.

Joanne's recorder was split in two.

And Jean-Pierre's hockey stick. Completely ruined!

No one could play basketball anymore...

... or drive safely.

This can't go
on any longer.

It's way too
dangerous!

It must have been someone using something sharp.

Was it Jonah with his new children's knife?

Or the hairdresser with his pair of scissors?

Or maybe Melvin with his sword?

The captain knew who had done it!
It was the lumberjack with his axe.

No,
it was not me!
Your mast seems
to have been
gnawed!

If it was not the lumberjack, then who was it?
A brave police officer went to investigate.

He
searched
and
searched
and
searched.

And then he saw...

... a
BEAVER!

A beaver had chewed through everything!

The officer took the bothersome beaver straight to jail.

But what bad luck!
The beaver chomped through the bars of his cell.

Then, the beaver struck again.
He could not be stopped!

Just act normal,
Buddy!

One little girl had a better idea.
She would just ask him to stop.

Hello, beaver.
Could you please
stop gnawing at
everything?

Oh, sorry!

I did not know I was
bothering anyone.

The beaver returned to the forest and everything got back to normal.

Goodbye!

Well, almost everything.